For Mum, who gave me stories, and Dad, who gave me music
S. S.

For Sher
B. L.

Text copyright © 2012 by Sally Sutton
Illustrations copyright © 2012 by Brian Lovelock

First U.S. edition 2012

Library of Congress Cataloging-in-Publication Data is available.

Library of Congress Catalog Card Number pending

ISBN 978-0-7636-5830-4

CCP 16 15 14 13 12 11
10 9 8 7 6 5 4 3 2 1

Printed in Shenzhen, Guangdong, China

This book was typeset in Franklin Gothic Extra Bold Condensed.
The illustrations were done in pigmented inks.

Candlewick Press
99 Dover Street
Somerville, Massachusetts 02144

visit us at www.candlewick.com

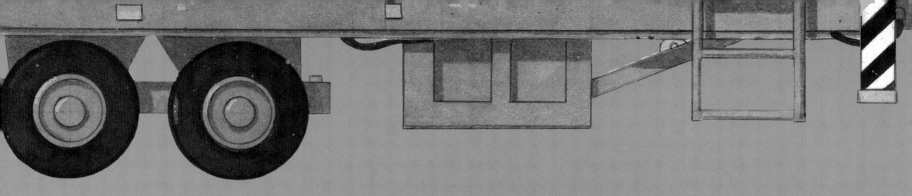

DEMOLITION

SALLY SUTTON · ILLUSTRATED BY BRIAN LOVELOCK

CANDLEWICK PRESS

Grab your gear. Grab your gear.

Buckle, tie, and strap.

Safety jackets, boots, and hats.

Swing the ball. Swing the ball.

Thump and smash and whack.

Bring the top floors tumbling down.

Bang! CLANG!

CRACK!

Work the jaws. Work the jaws.

Bite and tear and slash.

Dinosaurs had teeth like this!

Rip! ROAR!

CRASH!

Ram the walls. Ram the walls.

Bash and smash and slam.

First they wobble, then they fall.

Thud! CREAK! WHAM!

Hose the dust. Hose the dust.

Dampen down the dirt.

Careful, now! Don't cough or choke!

Whish! SPLISH! SQUIRT!

Crush the stone. Crush the stone.
Chip and grind and munch.
Make new concrete
from the old.

Shred the wood. Shred the wood.

Split and chop and chip.

Turn the sawdust into mulch.

Sort the steel. Sort the steel.
Heave and toss and bang.
Metal can be used again.

Load the trucks. Load the trucks.

Lift and shift and heap.

Drive away the piles of junk.

Whump! WHOP! BEEP!

Build the hut. Build the hut.

Tap and twist and knock.

Don't forget the monkey bars!

Join the fun. Join the fun.

Run and climb and play.

Give three cheers! The job is done.

Hip ... hip ...

HOORaY!

MACHINE FACTS

TRUCK: A truck takes material off the site.

WRECKING BALL: This heavy steel ball is hung from a crane and swung into the side of a building to smash it.

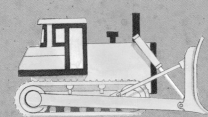

BULLDOZER: This bulldozer has a thick steel rake for ramming walls.

WOOD CHIPPER: A wood chipper shreds wood into sawdust, which can then be used as mulch for gardens.

HIGH-REACH EXCAVATOR: This excavator has a long boom arm, which can reach a tall building to pull it down.

MOBILE CRUSHER: A crusher grinds up broken concrete, which can be used to help make new concrete. Mobile crushers can be moved.

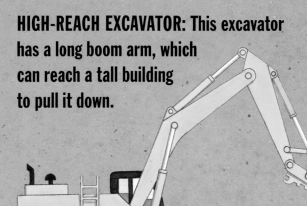

ROTATIONAL HYDRAULIC SHEARS: Rotational hydraulic shears can be attached to excavators to cut through concrete, steel, or wood.